الإوزّةُ التي باضتِ البيضةَ الذهبية

The Goose that laid the Golden Egg

Shaun Chatto ❖ Illustrated by Jago

Arabic translation
Wafa' Tarnowska

Mantra Lingua

كان يا مكان صيّادٌ يعيشُ في أقصى الغابة. كان أرملا ولم تكنْ له مطالبَ كثيرة. كان يطبخُ ما كانَ يجدْ – أرنباً بريّاً، أو فأرة. وفي أيام الأعياد اذا كان الحظُ قدْ حالفه، كان يطبخُ طائرَ الذيّال. عندما لم يكنْ قد تصيّدَ شيئاً، كانَ يأكلُ حساءَ الخضار.

في يومٍ من الأيامِ وجدَ الصيّادُ وزّةً تتمخترُ امامَ كوخه. ركضَ و راءَ الوزةِ من هنا وهناكَ حتى ألقى القبضَ عليها. ثم وضعَها في غرفةٍ وأخذَ يفتّش في كتابِ الطهيِ على طريقةِ طهيٍ مناسبة.

لكنَّ الركضَ وراءَ الوزةِ كانَ قد أتعبهُ فما لبثَ ان نام.

Once, there was a huntsman who lived deep in a forest. He was a widower and his needs were few. He would cook whatever he found – a hare, a mouse and on special days, if he was very lucky, even a pheasant. When he didn't catch anything, he had vegetable soup.
One day the huntsman found a goose wandering around outside his cottage. He chased the goose, here and there, until he finally caught her.
The huntsman bundled the goose into a room and then searched through his cookbook for a suitable recipe.
But all the running around had made him tired and he soon fell fast asleep.

في الصباحِ الباكرِ استيقظَ
الصيّادُ وأسرعَ الى الغرفةِ التي
كانت فيها الوزّةُ فرآها ساكنة
تغني لنفسِها بصوتٍ خافت.
وكانت بالقربِ منها بيضةٌ
كبيرةً تلمَع!

Early the next morning, the huntsman woke up
and rushed into the other room. There he found
the goose, quietly singing to herself. And next to
her was a large, glittering egg-shaped thing!

رفعَ الصيّادُ البيضةَ فكانت ثقيلة جداً ولم يشعرْ أنها بيضة عاديّة. هزّها لكنهُ لم يسمعْ صوتاً. بالطبعِ ما كانَ بامكانه انْ يأكلَ البيضةَ لانه لم يستطعْ كسرَ قشرتها القاسية. لم يعرفْ ماذا يفعلْ!

The huntsman picked it up. It was very heavy and did not feel like an ordinary egg. He shook it, but it didn't make a sound. He certainly couldn't eat it as there was no way he could crack the shiny hard shell. He just didn't know what to do!

بعدَ الظهرِ، ذهبَ الصيّادُ الى البلدةِ ليطلبَ المعونةَ من صديقه. نخزَ الصديقُ البيضةَ وحثّها ثم صاحَ باعجابٍ: "انها مصنوعة من الذهب الصلب"!

فأخذَ الصديقان البيضةَ الذهبيّةَ الى الصائغِ الذي دُهش برؤيةِ بيضةٍ ذهبيّة!

أعطى الصائغُ مالاً كثيراً للصيّادِ فتركَ الصديقان فرحان ثم عدّا المالَ وذهبا الى الخانِ المحليّ وطلبا وليمة كبيرة.

That afternoon, the huntsman journeyed to the town to ask his friend for help. His friend poked and prodded the egg-shaped thing. "It's – it's made of solid gold!" he cried in amazement.

So the two friends carried it to the jeweller who was astonished to see a golden egg!

She gave the huntsman a lot of money for it.

The friends went away, very happy. They counted out the money and then they had a feast at the local inn.

بعدَها كان يذهبُ الصيّادُ كلَّ صباحٍ الى الغرفةِ التي فيها الوزّة وكلَّ صباحٍ كان يجدُ الوزّةَ تغنّي لنفسها بصوتٍ خافتٍ وبقربها بيضة كبيرةً ذهبية!

أصبح الصيّادُ غنيّاً جداً اذْ كانَ يبيعُ البيضَ الذهبيَّ للصائغ الذي اغتنى أيضاً!

اشترى الصيّادُ لنفسهِ سريراً كبيراً مريحاً، وبنى حجرةً للمؤنِ أملاها بالطعامِ اللذيذ. ثم اشترى أيضاً كماناً اذ أصبحَ يتوفرُ لديه وقت كثير ولم يعد يلزمهُ ان يذهبَ الى الصيد.

Now each morning the huntsman rushed to the room where he kept the goose. And every morning he found the goose singing quietly to herself – and a large golden egg!
He became rich selling the eggs to the jeweller who also became wealthy!
The huntsman treated himself to a large comfortable bed. He got a bigger larder which he stocked with lots of delicious food. He also bought a violin, as he had lots of time on his hands, and he didn't need to go hunting any more.

لكنْ كسائرِ البشرِ لم يكنْ الصيادُ سعيداً بما لديهِ. أصبحَ
جشعاً وأخذ يطمعُ بأشياءَ أكثرَ وأكثر. أصبحَ قليلَ الصبرِ
ولم يعدْ يكتفي ببيضةٍ واحدةٍ في اليوم. أرادَ كلَّ البيضِ في
آنٍ واحدٍ!! لذلك فكّرَ الصيادُ بخطّة. دعا الوزّةَ الى المطبخ
واقترحَ عليها غناءَ اغنيةٍ معهِ. كانت الوزةُ فرحة جداً.
ولكنْ ما ان فتحَت فمَها...

But, like many people, the huntsman wasn't happy with
what he had. He became greedy, and wanted more and
more things.
He became impatient, and didn't want just one egg a day
– he wanted them all in one go!!
So the huntsman thought of a plan. He invited the goose
into his kitchen to sing a song together.
   The goose was delighted!
      But as soon as she opened her mouth ...

قطعها... قتل الصيادُ الوزّة. فتحَ بطنها بسرعةٍ آملاً ان يرى عدداً من البيضِ الذهبيّ

فيه. لكنه عندما تطلّعَ داخلَ بطنِ الوزّة لم يرى شيئا، لم يرى ايّ شيئ الا امعائها!

لم يرى بيضاً ذهبياً!

فجلس الصيادُ وبكى قائلاً: "لماذا، لماذا قتلتُ الوزّةَ التي كانتْ تبيضُ البيضَ الذهبيّ؟"

CHOP!
The huntsman killed the goose.
He quickly cut her open, expecting to find many more golden eggs.
But when he looked inside he found nothing, nothing but – her insides!
There were no golden eggs!
The huntsman sat down and wept, "Oh why have I killed the goose
that laid the golden eggs?"

Feelings (i) (?)

In *The Goose that Laid the Golden Egg*, the characters go through many different emotions as the story progresses. Think back to what happened in the story – can you work out which pictures below represent which emotion? Why not try retelling the story from the perspective of each character, using the thoughts and feelings that particular character might be experiencing.

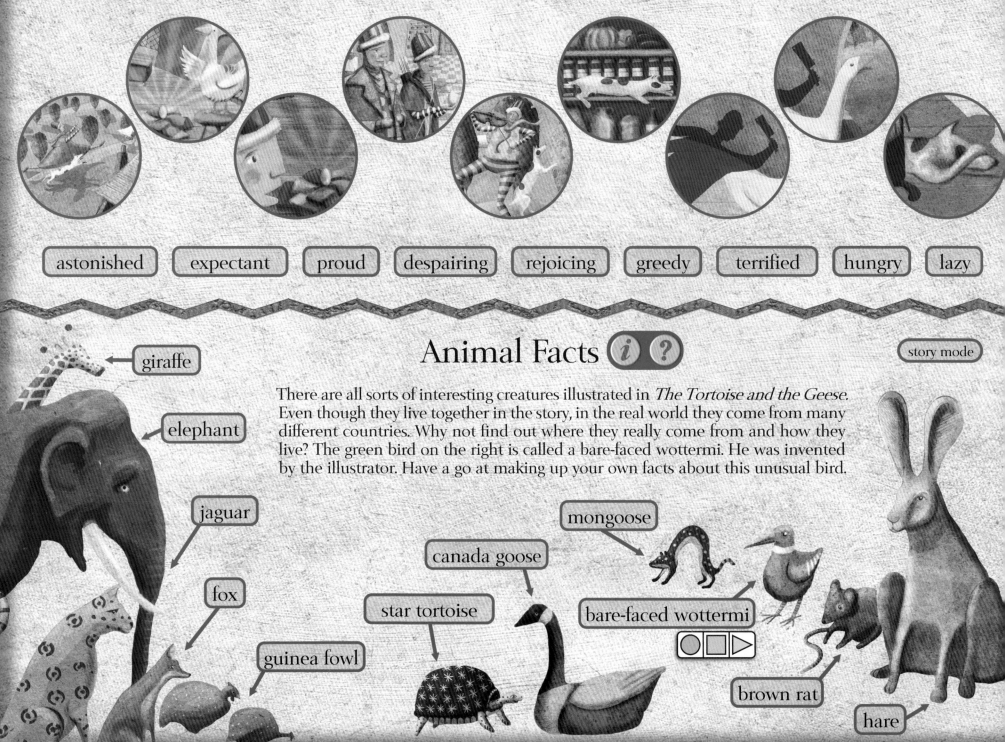

| astonished | expectant | proud | despairing | rejoicing | greedy | terrified | hungry | lazy |

Animal Facts (i) (?)

story mode

giraffe

There are all sorts of interesting creatures illustrated in *The Tortoise and the Geese*. Even though they live together in the story, in the real world they come from many different countries. Why not find out where they really come from and how they live? The green bird on the right is called a bare-faced wottermi. He was invented by the illustrator. Have a go at making up your own facts about this unusual bird.

elephant

jaguar

mongoose

fox

canada goose

star tortoise

bare-faced wottermi

guinea fowl

brown rat

hare

السلحفاةُ والوزّتان

The Tortoise and the Geese

كانت السلحفاةُ تعيشُ قربَ المستنقع منذُ زمنٍ طويل.

كلَّ صباحٍ كانت السلحفاةُ تجلسُ في ظلِّ شجرةِ البانيان، تقصُّ حكاياتٍ طويلةٍ غيرَ مترابطة معظمها عن نفسِها.

لم يكنْ للسلحفاةِ وقتًا لتستمعَ فيه الى الحيواناتِ الأخرى لذلك بدأتْ الحيواناتُ تتفاداها. لكنَّ السلحفاة لم تكفَّ عن الكلام. كانت تجلِسُ كلَّ يومٍ تقصُّ الحكايات والنكات امامَ جمهورٍ خياليّ. كانت الحيواناتُ الأخرى تلاحظ هذا الشيء فقالتْ: "الله يكون بعونِها! إنها قد جُنَّت!"

For as long as anyone could remember, the tortoise had lived by the pond. Every morning he could be found in the shade of the willow tree, telling long rambling stories, mostly about himself.
The tortoise never had any time to listen to the other animals and they soon began to avoid him. This didn't stop the tortoise from talking. Every day he would sit telling stories and jokes to an imaginary crowd.
The other animals saw this and said, "Poor thing! He's quite mad!"

في الخريف غطت وزّتان على المستنقعِ فوجدتا السلحفاةَ تكلّمُ نفسها: "كيف الحالُ يا جدّتي!" صاحت الوزّتان سويّاً. دارتُ السلحفاةُ رأسها وتطلعت بهنّ بعينانِ حزينتان.

"مرحباً" قالت السلحفاةُ بصوتٍ عميق يقعقع "ومن أنتما؟"

أجابتا: "نحن وزّتانِ إخوتان."

That autumn, a pair of young geese landed on the pond, where they saw the tortoise talking to himself. "Hi Granddad!" they chorused.
The tortoise turned and looked at them with woeful eyes. "Hello," he rumbled in his deep voice. "And who are you?"
"We are the Geese Brothers," they replied.

بعد بضعةِ أيامٍ تصادقَ الثلاثةُ وأصبحنَ أحسنَ الأصدقاءِ فرآهم الجميعُ يسبحنَ معاً في المستنقع.

Within a few days, the three became good friends and were often seen swimming together on the pond.

لكن حانَ وقتُ عودة الوزتان الى بلادهما فجاءت لتودّعا السلحفاة.
"ارجوكما، خذوني معكما،" ترجّت السلحفاة.
"لكنكِ لا تستطيعي الطيرانَ يا جدتّي،" قالت الوزتانِ بتعجّب.

"لديّ فكرة بارعة،" همَسَتْ السلحفاة. "إذ استطعتما حَملَ قضيبِ الخشبِ هذا بأرجلكما سأتعلّقُ
به بفمي. لذلك عندما تطيرا ستحملاني معكما!"

"أنها لفكرة عظيمة جداً،" اجابت الوزتان.

But all too soon it was time for the geese to return home, and they came to say goodbye to the tortoise.
"Please take me with you," pleaded the tortoise.
"But you can't fly, Granddad!" replied the amazed geese.
"I have a cunning plan," whispered the tortoise. "If the two of you can hold this piece of wood, I shall hang onto it with my mouth. When you fly off, you will be carrying me too!"
"What a clever plan," said the Geese Brothers.

عندَ يومِ السفرِ كان الخبرُ قد شاعَ فجاءت كلُّ
الحيواناتِ لتودّعَ السلحفاة. كانت كلها حزينة
لأن السلحفاة كانت تعيشُ قرب المستنقع منذ
مدّة طويلة جداً.

On the day of departure, word had spread and all
the animals gathered to say goodbye. They were a
little bit sad. After all, the tortoise had lived there
for EVER.

حملت الوزتان قضيبَ الخشبِ بأرجلهما بينما تعلّقت
به السلحفاةُ بفمها. ثم طارتِ الوزتان في السماءِ عالياً
والسلحفاةُ معلّقة بالخشبة. دُهِشَتْ الحيوانات الأخرى
عندما رأتْ هذا المنظرَ العجيب!

The Geese Brothers held the piece of wood with their feet. The tortoise gripped
it firmly in his mouth. With a whoosh the Geese Brothers flew up into the sky,
with the tortoise dangling from the wood. The other animals gasped as they
saw this amazing sight!

طارت الحيواناتُ الثلاثةُ فوقَ حقولٍ خضراءَ مزيّنة بالشجر والبحيرات،
حيث الرياحُ تدفعُ القوارب.
طارتِ الحيواناتُ الثلاثةُ فوقَ غاباتٍ داكنة وجبالٍ عالية. لم تكن
السلحفاةُ قد سافرت قطّ لذلك كانت تتطلّعُ بدهشة.

ما أوسعَ وأجملَ العالم وكلَ ما فيه! أحست بسعادةٍ لأن فكرتها كانت قد
نجحت حقاً.

The trio were soon flying over green fields dotted with
trees, and lakes where sailboats glided gently in the
wind. They flew over dark forests and high mountains.
The tortoise had never been abroad and he
watched in amazement. What a large and
wonderful world there was to see!
He felt quite pleased that his little plan
had worked so well.

بعد مدّةٍ، طارت الحيواناتُ فوقَ مدينةٍ كبيرة. كان بعضُ الأطفال يلعبون في الحديقةِ العامةِ فتطلعوا الى الأعلى وقالوا، "أنظري يا أمّي، سلحفاة تطير!"
"هش يا أولاد..." قالت الامُ، ثم رأت هي أيضاً السلحفاةَ الطائرةَ وفتحت فمها بدهشة.
ثم انضمَ اليها آخرون وتجمّعَ حشدٌ أخذ يدلُّ الى السماءِ ويصفق ويصيح.

After a while they flew over a large city.
Some children playing in a park looked up and gasped, "Look Mum – a flying tortoise!"
"Hush dear ..." the mother started to say, and then she too saw the flying tortoise and her jaw dropped.
Soon others joined them and a crowd gathered, all pointing to the sky, clapping and cheering.

سمِعَتْ السلحفاةُ الضجّة المنبعِثة من الأرضِ ورأت الناسَ
يدلّون عليها بأصابعهم. تضايقت السلحفاة. ظنت أن الناسَ
تضحكُ عليها فقررت أن تعلنَ لهم عن رأيها.

The tortoise heard the hullabaloo down below and saw the people pointing their
fingers in his direction. The tortoise felt annoyed. He thought they were making
fun of him and so he decided to tell them what he thought.

فتحت السلحفاةُ فمها... فأفلتت
قضيبَ الخشب... فوقعت!

The tortoise opened his mouth ...
lost his grip ... and fell!

"ساعدووووني!" صرخت
وهي تتساقطُ في الفضاء.

"Heelpp!" he screamed, as he
hurtled through the air.

هبطتِ السلحفاةُ بشدّة على دغلٍ كبيرٍ مورقٍ حيثُ كان
أرنبٌ بريٌّ يستريحُ بعد الظهر.
"كنتِ قد قتلتِني!" صاحَ الأرنبُ البرّي.
"قتلتُك؟ كيف نقولُ قتلتُكَ...؟" صاحتِ السلحفاة.
ثمّ توقّفتْ وفكّرت...

The tortoise landed heavily on a large leafy bush where a hare
was having his afternoon siesta.
"You could have killed me!" screamed the startled hare.
"Killed you? What do you mean killed *you* ...?" the tortoise shouted back.
Then he stopped, and he thought ...

ثم عندما فتحت فمَها مرّةً ثانية تكلّمت بلطفٍ وقالت: "أعذرني سيّدي الارنب
أحيانًا أتكلمُ بدونِ تفكيرٍ لذلِكَ هبطتُ عليك."

And when he next opened his mouth, he spoke softly, "I'm sorry Mr Hare, sometimes I talk without thinking and that's why I landed on you."

"ما اللذي حصل؟" سألَ الأرنبُ البرّي.
"انها لقصةٌ طويلة،" اجابت السلحفاة،
"لكنْ اذا كنتَ حقيقةً تريدُ معرفتها،
يسرُّني أن أخبرَكَ إياها."

"What happened?" asked the hare.
"Well, that's a long story," said the tortoise, "but if you *really*
want to know, I will be happy to tell you."

Tell your own Goose Fable!

The Goose that Laid the Golden Egg

The Tortoise and the Geese